My Sister is *My Sister!*

Leslie Clark

ISBN: 979-8-9870138-1-6
Printed in the U.S.A

To all the blended families navigating unique family dynamics daily...

"We ain't picture perfect but we worth the picture still." – J.Cole

A special thank you to my kids, Elise and Camden; thank you for teaching me unconditional love and the true meaning of family.

Families are all different.
And I know this is true.

They may use different names for things.
But for me, only one will do.

There is bonus, step,
and sometimes half...
just to name a few.

But My Sister is *My Sister,*
and that's the only one that will do.

Our moms
may be
different,
but our
dad is
the same.

So it is very
easy to find
a name for
us to claim.

Our parents put us
first and make
sure we spend
time together.

They make sure
we have great memories
that we will
always treasure.

School
We go to
different schools,
School
and that is
quite okay.

I look forward to seeing her on the weekends so that we can play.

Whenever we are together
it's always a ton of fun.

Dad is always watching.
He is so proud of his daughters and what they have become!

Saying our goodbyes
is always hard to do.

I rush to my calender
to mark the
next time that
I will see you.

Time can
sometimes pass,
but the love
remains the same.

My Sister is
My Sister,
and that will
never change.

So when they ask about you,
which I'm sure they will do.

There is only one thing to say:
My Sister is *My Sister!*

I love her. Yes, I do!